Walt Disney's
version of
PINOCCHIO

WITH AN INTRODUCTION BY MAURICE SENDAK

HARRY N. ABRAMS, INC., *Publishers*, NEW YORK

Editor: Darlene Geis

I've Got No Strings, Little Woodenhead, and *Give A Little Whistle*
Words by Ned Washington, music by Leigh Harline. Copyright © 1940
Bourne Co. Copyright renewed. International copyright secured.
All rights reserved. Used by permission.

"Walt Disney/2" from CALDECOTT & CO. by Maurice Sendak. Copyright
© 1988 by Maurice Sendak. Reprinted by permission of Farrar,
Straus and Giroux, Inc.

Library of Congress Cataloging-in-Publication Data
Walt Disney's version of Pinocchio.
    Walt Disney's Pinocchio.
        p.   cm.
    Reprint. Originally Published: Walt Disney's version of Pinocchio.
New York: Random House, 1939.
    Based on the story by Collodi, with illustrations from the motion
picture.
    Summary: The adventures of the wooden puppet boy whose nose grew
whenever he told a lie.
    ISBN 0-8109-1467-0
    [1. Fairy tales. 2. Puppets—Fiction.] I. Collodi, Carlo,
1826–1890. Avventure di Pinocchio.   II. Title.
PZ8.P66   1989
[Fic]—dc19   88–39260

This facsimile of the original 1939 edition is published in 1989 by
Harry N. Abrams, Incorporated, New York. All rights reserved.
No part of the contents of this book may be reproduced without the
written permission of the publisher

A Times Mirror Company

Printed and bound in Japan

WALT DISNEY'S TRIUMPH:

THE ART OF *PINOCCHIO*

by Maurice Sendak

T IS the winter of 1940. The world is five months into a new war and I am very aware that it is wrong to be happy. But I am. I have been promised a trip uptown to see Walt Disney's new film, *Pinocchio*, and my only concern is not being late. It is roughly an hour from Brooklyn to midtown Manhattan on the BMT, and my sister and her girl friend are, as usual, dragging their feet. It is just another example of the awfulness of children's dependence on the adult world to fulfill their most desperate wishes.

By the time we reach the theater, I have lost what little self-control I had left. The movie had already begun. I go into a black sulk and my sister, furious, threatens to abandon me altogether. We climb to the balcony in angry silence and clamber across an invisible and endless row of knees to our seats. The sound track, in the meantime, fills the dark with the most irresistible music. I can't bear to look at the screen. I have missed, I feel, the best of everything. But my first glimpse once past the 4,000th knee dissipates all my anguish. Jiminy Cricket is sliding jauntily down the strings of a violin, singing "Give a Little Whistle." (The scene occurs 20 minutes into the film; I've clocked it often since that day.) I was happy then and have remained forever happy in the memory of *Pinocchio*.

If remembering that day is tinged with a confusing guilt that has something to do with the inappropriateness of feeling cheerful when a world war was hanging over our heads, then that, too, is part of the precious memory of *Pinocchio*. I was only a child, but I knew something dreadful was happening in the world, and that my parents were worried to death. And it seems to me that something of the quality of that terrible, anxious time is reflected in the very color and dramatic power of *Pinocchio*. Certainly, it is the darkest of all Disney films. This is not to deny that it is also a charming, amusing, and touching film. It is, however, rooted in melancholy, and in this respect it is true to the original Italian tale. But that is where any significant resemblance between Disney and Collodi ends.

Disney has often been condemned for corrupting the classics, and he has, to be sure, occasionally slipped in matters of taste and absolute fidelity to the original. But he has never corrupted. If there have been errors, they are nothing compared to the violations against the true nature and psychology of children committed by some of the so-called classics. C. Collodi's *Pinocchio*, first published in 1883, is a case in point. As a child, I disliked it. When I grew up, I wondered if perhaps my early dislike was ill founded. My memory of the book was a mixture of the utterly sad and the peculiarly unpleasant; and when I finally reread it, I found that this memory is accurate. While Collodi's *Pinocchio* is an undeniably engaging narrative that moves with tremendous energy—despite its shaky, loose construction—it is also a cruel and frightening tale. It does not suffer from whimsicality or sentimentality, but its premise is sickening.

Children, Collodi appears to be saying, are inherently bad, and the world itself is a ruthless, joyless place, filled with hypocrites, liars, and cheats. Poor Pinocchio is *born* bad. While still mostly a block of firewood—just his head and hands are carved—he is already atrocious, instantly using those new hands to abuse his wood-carver papa, Geppetto. Only moments after Pinocchio's creation, Geppetto is wiping tears from his eyes and regretting the marionette's existence: "I should have thought of this before I made him. Now it is too late!" Pinocchio doesn't stand a chance; he is evil incarnate—a happy-go-lucky ragazzo—but damned nevertheless.

In order to grow into boyhood, Pinocchio has to yield up his own self entirely, unquestioningly, to his father—and, later in the book, to the strange lady with the azure hair (the Blue Fairy of the film). When that elusive lady promises to be Pinocchio's mother, there is this nasty hook attached: "You will obey me always and do as I wish?" Pinocchio promises that he will. She then delivers a dreary sermon, ending: "Laziness is a serious illness and one must cure it immediately; yes, even from early childhood. If not, it will kill you in the end." No wonder Pinocchio soon disobeys. His instincts warn him off and he runs away, apparently preferring laziness and wickedness to the castrating love of this hard-hearted fairy. It's a strange paradox that Collodi equates becoming "a real boy" with turning into a capon.

At its best, the book has moments of mad black humor, with more than a touch of Woody Allenish logic. When Pinocchio first meets the fairy, for instance, he is trying to escape from assassins who mean to rob and kill him. He knocks frantically on her door, and she appears at her window, with "a face white as wax," to tell him that everyone in the house, herself included, is dead. "Dead?" Pinocchio screams in fury. "What are you doing at the window, then?" That is Pinocchio's true voice. This hilarious, nightmarish scene ends with the exasperating lovely lady leaving the marionette to the mercy of the assassins—who hang him from a giant oak tree. The story is full of such ghastly, sadistic moments, most of them not funny at all.

So far as I am concerned, Collodi's book is of interest today chiefly as evidence of the superiority of Disney's screenplay. The Pinocchio in the film is not the unruly, sulking, vicious, devious (albeit still charming) marionette that Collodi created. Neither is he an innately evil, doomed-to-calamity child of sin. He is, rather, both lovable and loved. Therein lies Disney's triumph. His Pinocchio is a mischievous, innocent, and very naive little wooden boy. What makes our anxiety over his fate endurable is a reassuring sense that Pinocchio is loved for himself—and not for what he should or shouldn't be. Disney has corrected a terrible wrong. Pinocchio, he says, is good; his "badness" is only a matter of inexperience.

Nor is Disney's Jiminy Cricket the boring, browbeating preacher/cricket he is in the book (so boring that even Pinocchio brains him). In the movie, we watch Jiminy's intelligent curiosity concerning the marionette quicken into genuine interest and affection. He is a loyal though not uncritical friend, and his flip and sassy ways do not diminish our faith in his reliability. Despite his failure to convince Pinocchio of the difference between right and wrong, his willingness to understand and forgive the puppet's foolish waywardness makes him a complicated cricket indeed. The Blue Fairy is still a bit stuffy about the virtues of truth and honesty, but she can laugh and is as quick as Jiminy to forgive. Who could fail to forgive inexperience?

Disney has deftly pulled the story together and made a tight dramatic structure out of the rambling sequence of events in the Collodi book. Pinocchio's wish to be a real boy remains the film's underlying theme, but "becoming a real boy" now signifies the wish to grow up, not the wish to be good. Our greatest fear is that he may not make his way safely through the mine fields of his various adventures to get what, finally, he truly deserves. We still miss the little wooden boy at the end of the film (there is just no way of loving the flesh-and-blood boy as much as we did the marionette), but we are justifiably happy for Pinocchio. His wish to be a real boy is as passionate and believable a longing as is Dorothy's wish, in the film version of L. Frank Baum's *The Wizard of Oz*, to find her way home to Kansas. Both Pinocchio and Dorothy deserve to have their wishes come true; they prove themselves more than worthy. Oddly, both of these movies are superior to the "classics" that inspired them.

About two years were devoted to the production of *Pinocchio*, easily the best of the Disney films, as well as the most fearless and emotionally charged. Some 500,000 drawings appear on the screen, and this does not include tens of thousands of preliminary drawings, story sketches, atmosphere sketches, layouts, character models, and stage settings. Extensive use of the Disney-developed multiplane camera—first tried out in *Snow White*—allows for ingenious camera movement similar to the dolly shots of live movie production. According to Christopher Finch in his 1973 book *The Art of Walt Disney*: "A single scene in which the camera zooms down on the village with the school bells ringing and the pigeons circling down until they are among the houses cost $45,000 (equivalent to perhaps $200,000 today). The scene lasts only a few seconds. . . . The result was an animated movie of unprecedented lavishness." The production details are overwhelming, but in the end they are only statistics. After half a century, the movie itself is the vital proof that all that manpower, machinery, and money went into creating a work of extraordinary skill, beauty, and mystery. And if there are flaws—and there are—the sheer force of originality easily compensates for them. If I wish the Blue Fairy didn't remind me of a typical '30s movie queen, and Cleo, the goldfish, of a miniature, underwater mix of Mae West and Carmen Miranda, this merely acknowledges that even masterpieces have their imperfections.

As for those tantalizing 20 minutes I missed back in February 1940, I have since seen them again and again, though that never makes up for missing them the first time. The movie contains so many memorable episodes; for example, the one in which Jiminy and Pinocchio converse in bubbling speech as they move about the ocean floor, looking for Monstro, the whale, and the swallowed Geppetto. And, near the end of the Pleasure Island sequence, there is the starkly terrifying scene in which Pinocchio's new friend, Lampwick, turns into a donkey. It starts amusingly enough, but Lampwick's growing alarm and then outright hysteria quickly become painful. His flailing arms turn into hoofs, and his last awful cry of *Ma-Ma*, as his shadow on the wall collapses onto all fours, makes us realize that he is lost forever.

After the dramatic ocean chase, when the vengeful Monstro tries to destroy Geppetto and Pinocchio, we see with relief the old wood-carver washed up on shore and Figaro, the cat, and Cleo in her bowl washed up beside him. A bedraggled Jiminy arrives next, calling for Pinocchio. Then the camera leaps to a shot of the marionette, face down in a pool of water: dead. That image, for me, is the most shocking in the whole film. Pinocchio has forfeited his life to save his father. Coming only moments later, in the funeral scene, is the Blue Fairy's reward. She revives the brave marionette into a new life as a real boy. Tactfully, we are not permitted to dwell too long on his ordinary, little boy's face.

Watching *Pinocchio* now, I am inevitably struck by a sense of regret—of loss. It would almost certainly be impossible to finance such an enterprise today. The movie has the golden glamour of a lost era; it is a monument to an age of craft and quality in America. It is too easy to shrug and say the money isn't there anymore. In my own business of publishing one watches with growing dismay the ersatz quality of bookmaking, the vanishing forever of traditional linotype faces, and the degeneration of paper. Over the past few decades, there has been a collapse of the sense of pride in craftsmanship, of the sense of excellence. Usually, this has nothing to do with money. A rough, early Mickey Mouse short—any one of them!—is superior to the animation that is currently manufactured for television. We are in the dark McDonald's age of the quick and easy. *Pinocchio* is a shining reminder of what once was—of what could be again.

THIS IS the book version of our second feature-length animated motion picture, Pinocchio, based on the famous Collodi story of the mischievous wooden puppet who comes to life and goes through amazing adventures.

It is dedicated to the many people, young and old, whose encouraging letters suggested that we tell the story of Pinocchio in our medium.

The illustrations by the studio staff are original production drawings created during the two years our picture was in the making.

Walt Disney

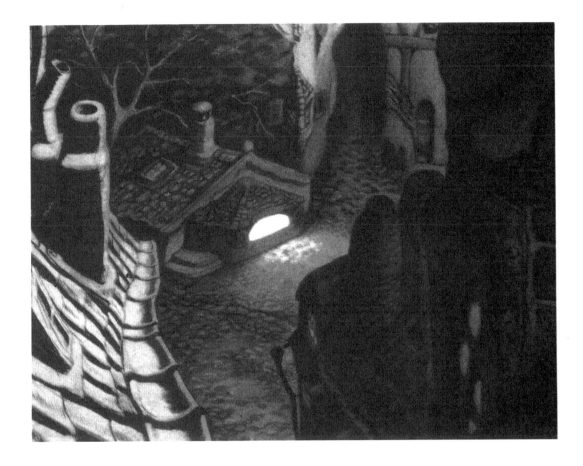

ONE NIGHT long, long ago, the Evening Star shone down across the dark sky. Its beams formed a shimmering pathway to a tiny village, and painted its humble roofs with stardust.

But the silent little town was deep in sleep. The only witness to the beauty of the night was a weary wayfarer who chanced to be passing through.

His clothes were gray with dust. His well-worn shoes pinched his feet; his back ached from the weight of the carpetbag slung over his shabby shoulder. To be

sure, it was only a small carpetbag; but this wayfarer had a very small shoulder. As a matter of fact, he was an exceedingly small wayfarer. His name was Cricket. Jiminy Cricket.

He marveled at the radiant star; it seemed almost close enough to touch, and pretty as a picture. But at this moment Jiminy Cricket was not interested in pretty pictures. He was looking for a place to rest.

Suddenly he noticed a light in a window, and smoke curling from a chimney.

"Where there's smoke, there's a fire," he reasoned. "Where there's a fire, there's a hearth. And where there's a hearth, there *should* be a cricket!"

And with that, he hopped up to the window sill and peered in. The room had a friendly look. So Jiminy crawled under the door, scurried over to the hearth, backed up against the glowing fireplace, and warmed his little britches.

It was no ordinary village home into which the small wayfarer had stumbled. It was a workshop: the workshop of Geppetto the woodcarver. Old Geppetto was working late that night. He was making a puppet.

Geppetto lived alone except for his black kitten, Figaro, and a pet goldfish he called Cleo. But he had many friends; everyone knew and loved the kindly, white-haired old man. He had spent his whole life creating happiness for others.

It was the children who loved Geppetto best. He doctored their dolls, put clean sawdust into limp rag bodies and painted fresh smiles on faded china faces. He fashioned new arms and legs for battered tin soldiers — and there was magic in his hands when he carved a toy.

Though he seemed poor, Geppetto's tiny shop (which was also his home) was crowded with priceless treasures. Wonderfully carved canes, unique clocks, music boxes, decorated with quaint wooden figures so lifelike that Geppetto sometimes talked to them as though they were real. And playthings fit for the Christmas stocking of a prince!

Now the weary old fellow put his tools away and surveyed his newest handiwork. The puppet was jointed and strung; all that remained was to paint the wooden face.

The puppet had the figure of a small boy. He was the right size for a small boy. He had the cute, round face of a small boy – except for one feature. The nose! Geppetto had given him a very long and pointed nose, such a nose as no real boy ever possessed. A funny nose.

The old woodcarver stroked his chin and chuckled.

"Well, Figaro," he said to the kitten, "little Woodenhead is nearly finished. How do you like him?"

But Figaro only blinked his yellow eyes and yawned. To tell the truth, he was jealous of the puppet because Geppetto liked it so much. Geppetto patted him affectionately.

"Soon we will go to bed, Figaro," he promised the drowsy kitten. "But first I must paint this funny face."

He dipped his brush in water, pulling it out hastily — for by mistake, he had dipped it into Cleo's bowl. The goldfish acted offended until Geppetto apologized; but then she seemed to forgive him in her own quaint way.

Next Geppetto carefully painted a little turned-down mouth on the wooden face. Figaro and Cleo both frowned and shook their heads, so Geppetto rubbed the scowl off.

"Even on a clown that's made of wood, a little wooden frown is not so good," he commented. "Wear a happy, joyful smile instead! That's better, little Woodenhead!" For now the puppet, Figaro and Cleo were all smiling.

There was something unusual about that wooden marionette — something that made you look twice. He looked almost like a real boy, even though he was just wood and strings.

"Woodenhead," Geppetto exclaimed proudly, "you deserve a name. What shall I call you? I know—*Pinocchio!* Do you like it?" He worked the puppet's strings so that it nodded "Yes."

"That settles it!" cried Geppetto happily. "Pinocchio you are! And now we will try you out! Music, Professor —"

Jiminy Cricket, who was watching with great interest, stared around and saw that the "Professor" was a little wood figure of an orchestra conductor, carved on a music box!

Geppetto pushed a button. The professor waved a baton, the music box began to tinkle, and small wooden musicians began to saw and toot on tiny instruments. Then, by working his strings, Geppetto made Pinocchio dance.

As he did so he sang, making up words to fit the tune.
"Little Woodenhead all made of pine,
Little wooden boy with eyes that shine,
Little wooden toes that just won't grow,
A little wooden nose that just won't blow . . .
Little wooden feet, and best of all —
A little wooden seat, in case you *fall* —"
Geppetto made the puppet sit down suddenly, and

laughed heartily at his joke. The dance was over.

  Still the lonely old man could not bring himself to call it a day. Suddenly his many clocks began to strike. The air was filled with clock  sounds — cuckoos, buzzing bees, barking dogs, honking ducks, bells. Each clock said "Nine o'clock" in its own special way. Geppetto sighed and put the puppet down.

       "Time for bed," he yawned. "Good-night, Figaro! Good-night, Cleo!"

JIMINY Cricket was glad to hear these words, for he felt very sleepy. Geppetto put on a long white nightshirt and climbed creakily into bed, but he still sat admiring the

puppet with its wooden smile.

"Look at him, Figaro!" he exclaimed. "He seems almost real. Wouldn't it be nice if he were alive?"

But the only answer from the kitten was a snore, so the lonely old fellow settled himself for sleep.

For a moment all was quiet. Then Geppetto remembered the window was still closed. He sighed and woke Figaro to open it. Through the casement, they saw the Evening Star.

"The Wishing Star!" whispered Geppetto.

Then he knelt like a child, clasped his hands and said:

"Star light, star bright —
First star I've seen tonight.
I wish I may — I wish I might —
Have the wish I wish tonight!"

He turned to his wooden puppet. "Pinocchio," he said, "I wish you were a real boy."

Long after Geppetto had gone to sleep, Jiminy Cricket lay awake thinking. It made him sad to realize the old man's wish could never come true, and tired as he was, the little fellow could not sleep.

Suddenly he heard something. Music—mysterious music! He sat up and looked around the room. Then he saw a strange light — a brilliant glow, which grew more dazzling every minute. It was the star — the Evening Star, floating down the sky and entering Geppetto's window!

Then in the center of its blinding glow appeared a very beautiful lady dressed in robes of flowing blue.

"As I live and breathe!" Jiminy whispered in astonishment. "A fairy!" For in her hand he saw a wand tipped with a shining star.

The beautiful lady was none other than the Blue Fairy, whose work it is to see that people are rewarded for their good deeds. She is really the nicest of all fairies. She came tonight in answer to Geppetto's wish.

She leaned over the old woodcarver and spoke to him ever so softly, so as not to disturb his slumber.

"Good Geppetto," she said, "you have given so much happiness to others, you deserve to have your wish come true!"

Then she turned to the wooden puppet. Reaching out her glittering wand, she spoke these words:

"Little puppet made of pine,
Wake! The gift of life is thine!"

And when the wand touched him, Pinocchio came to life! First he blinked his eyes, then

he raised his wooden arm and wiggled his jointed fingers.

"I can move!" he cried joyfully. "I can *talk!*"

"Yes, Pinocchio," the Blue Fairy smiled. "Geppetto needs a little son. So tonight I give you life."

"Then I'm a real boy!" cried Pinocchio joyfully.

"No," said the Fairy sadly. "There is no magic that can make us real. I have given you life — the rest is up to you."

"Tell me what I must do," begged Pinocchio. "I want to be a real boy!"

"Prove yourself brave, truthful, and unselfish," said the Blue Fairy. "Be a good son to Geppetto — make him proud of you! Then, some day, you will wake up and find yourself a real boy!"

"Whew! That won't be easy," thought Jiminy Cricket.

But the Blue Fairy also realized what a hard task she was giving Pinocchio. "The world is full of temptations," she continued.

"You must learn to choose between right and wrong—"

"Right? Wrong?" questioned Pinocchio. "How will I know?"

Jiminy wrung his hands in desperation. But the wise Fairy was not yet finished. "Your conscience will tell you the difference between right and wrong," she explained.

"Conscience?" Pinocchio repeated. "What are conscience?"

That was too much for Jiminy Cricket. He hopped down where he could be seen.

"A conscience," he shouted, "is that still small voice people won't listen to! That's the trouble with the world today!"

"Are *you* my conscience?" asked Pinocchio eagerly.

Jiminy was embarrassed, but the Blue Fairy came to his rescue. "Would you like to be Pinocchio's conscience?" she smiled. "You seem a man of the world. What is your name?"

Jiminy was flattered. "Jiminy Cricket," he answered.

"Kneel, Mister Cricket," commanded the Blue Fairy.

Jiminy knelt and trembled as her wand touched him.

"I dub you Pinocchio's conscience," she proclaimed, "Lord High Keeper of the Knowledge of Right and Wrong! Arise—*Sir* Jiminy Cricket!"

And when the dusty little cricket rose his shabby old clothes were gone and he was clad in elegant raiment from head to foot.

"Don't I get a badge or something?" he asked.

"We'll see," the Blue Fairy smiled.

"Make it a gold one?" urged Jiminy.

"Perhaps, if you do your job well," she said. "I leave Pinocchio in your hands. Give him the benefit of your advice and experience. Help him to be a real boy!"

It was a serious moment for the little cricket. He promised to help Pinocchio as much as he could, and to stick by him through thick and thin. The Blue Fairy thanked him.

"And now, Pinocchio," she said, "be a good boy — and always let your conscience be your guide! Don't be discouraged because you are different from the other boys! Remember — *any child who is not good, might just as well be made of wood!*"

The Blue Fairy backed slowly away. There was one last soft chord of music and she was gone.

 **P**INOCCHIO and Jiminy stared silently at the spot where the Fairy had stood, half hoping she might return. The

little cricket finally broke the spell.

"Say, she's all right, son!" he exclaimed. "Remember what she told you — always let your conscience be your guide!"

"Yes, sir, I will!" answered Pinocchio.

"And when you need me, whistle," said Jiminy, "like this!"

"Like this?" Pinocchio tried, but no sound came.

So Jiminy sang him a little lecture-lesson, which went something like this:

"When you get in trouble
And you don't know right from wrong,
Give a little whistle
Give a little whistle
When you meet temptation
And the urge is very strong,
Give a little whistle
Give a little whistle."

Then he began dancing down the strings of a violin on the bench, balancing himself with his small umbrella.

"Take the straight and narrow path
And if you start to slide,
Give a little whistle
Give a little whistle — "

Just then the violin string broke. Jiminy fell over backward, but picked himself up and finished, "and always let your conscience be your guide!"

Pinocchio watched entranced as the little cricket went on dancing. Finally he too jumped up and tried to make his wooden feet go through the same steps. But he danced too close to the edge of the work bench, lost his balance and fell clatteringly to the floor.

The noise woke Geppetto. "Who's there?" he called. Pinocchio, on the floor, answered, "It's *me!*"

Geppetto's teeth chattered with fright. "Figaro, there's somebody in here!" he whispered. "A burglar, maybe! Come, we'll catch him!"

Then to his surprise, he noticed his puppet, which he had left on the workbench, lying on the floor.

"Why, Pinocchio!" he exclaimed, "how did you get down there?" He picked the puppet up and set him back on

the bench. Imagine his surprise when Pinocchio answered!

"I fell down," he said.

Geppetto stared. "What! You're talking?" he cried. "No! You're only a marionette. You can't talk!"

"Yes, I can," insisted the puppet. "I can move, too!"

The old man backed away. "No, no," he argued. "I must be dreaming! I will pour water on myself! I will stick me with pins!"

Geppetto made sure he was awake. "Now we will see who is dreaming," he challenged. "Go on — say something!"

Pinocchio laughed merrily. "Do it again!" he begged. "You're awful funny! I like you!"

"You *do* talk," said the old man, in a

hushed voice. "Pinocchio! It's a miracle! Figaro! Cleo! Look — he's alive!"

Geppetto didn't know whether to laugh or cry, he was so happy. "This calls for a celebration!" he announced. He turned on a music box and began to dance. He went to his toy shelves and filled his arms with playthings. It was just like Christmas for Pinocchio. He couldn't decide which toy to play with first!

But the music box ran down and the celebration ended.

"Now it is time for bed," said the old woodcarver. "Come, Pinocchio. You shall sleep here in this dresser drawer."

He went to get something for Pinocchio to sleep in. Just then Pinocchio noticed a new toy — the burning candle. He thought the flame was pretty, and reached out to pick it up. One of his wooden fingers caught fire. He was very pleased.

"Look!" he exclaimed. "Pretty!"

"Help, help!" Geppetto cried, picking Pinocchio up in his arms. He plunged the burning finger into the goldfish bowl, the flame sizzled and went out.

"Why, Pinocchio," he scolded. "You must never play with fire!"

"Why not?" Pinocchio asked.

"Because you are made of wood," Geppetto chuckled. "But never mind. Go to sleep — it's late. Sleep fast, Pinocchio!"

That night, Jiminy Cricket did an unusual thing — for him. He prayed. He prayed that Pinocchio might never disappoint that kind, happy old man or the lovely Blue Fairy, and that he might be a good conscience, so Pinocchio would soon earn the right to be a real boy.

All was still in the little shop. High in the sky the Evening Star twinkled softly, as though smiling approval of a good night's work.

ORNING dawned bright and clear. As the school bells rang out over the village, their clamor sent

pigeons flying from the old belfrey like colored fans spread against the white clouds.

The school bells carried a special message of joy to old Geppetto. Today his own son was to join the other little ones on their way to school!

Pinocchio too was impatient. His face, shiny from scrub-

bing, beamed with excitement. Even Figaro and Cleo realized it was a gala day.

At last Pinocchio was pronounced ready. Geppetto opened the door. For the first time the puppet looked out at the wide, wide world. How beautiful it was! "What are those?" he asked, pointing down the street. "Those are the children, bless them!" Geppetto answered. "They are the boys and girls—your schoolmates, Pinocchio!"

"Real boys?" Pinocchio asked eagerly.

"Yes, my son. And if you study hard, you'll soon be as smart as they are. Wait a minute — your books —"

Little Figaro appeared in the door, tugging at the strap which held Pinocchio's school books.

"Ah, thank you, Figaro. You too want to help! Pinocchio, here are your books. Remember: be a good boy.

Choose your friends carefully; shun evil companions. Mind the teacher —"

"Good-by!" shouted Pinocchio, pulling carelessly away. But he thought better of it, ran back and threw his arms around Geppetto. "Good-by, father," he said shyly; then off he marched, his books under his arm, chock-full of good resolutions.

Jiminy Cricket heard the school bell and jumped up in a great hurry. Suppose Pinocchio had gone off to school without him! If ever a small boy needed a conscience, it is on his first day at school. A fine time to oversleep, he thought. Then he stuffed his shirt hastily inside his trousers, grabbed his hat and rushed out.

"Hey, Pinoke!" he called cheerily. "Wait for me!"

GEPPETTO saw Pinocchio safely off to school, then went cheerily to his work bench.

"An extra mouth to feed, Figaro," he chuckled to the kitten. "Yet what a joy it is to have some one to work for!"

But alas, many a dreary day and night were to pass before the old woodcarver saw his boy again! For in spite of Geppetto's warning, Pinocchio fell into bad company. He met two scheming adventurers — a Fox and a Cat, the worst pair of scoundrels in the whole countryside.

Run down at the heel and patched at the seat, these villains managed somehow to look like elegant gentlemen out for a stroll. But as usual, they were up to no good.

Suddenly, "Look!" cried the sharp-eyed Fox, who went by the name of J. Worthington Foulfellow, alias Honest John. "Do you see what I see?" He pointed with his cane. The stupid Cat, who was called Gideon, stared at Pinocchio.

"A puppet that walks!" marveled Foulfellow. "A live puppet — a marionette without strings! Gideon," he whispered, dodging into a doorway, "that boy is worth a fortune to some one. Now *who* —" His roving eye fell on a poster stuck to a nearby signboard.

"*Stromboli's Marionette Show,*" the Fox read slowly. Then he snapped his fingers. "That's it!" he whispered. "We'll sell the puppet to Stromboli!"

Thus the villains plotted. As Pinocchio passed, the Fox put out his cane. Pinocchio tripped and fell.

"My dear young man! I'm so sorry," Foulfellow apologized, helping him to his feet. "A most regrettable accident — Mr. — er —"

"Pinocchio," answered the puppet cheerfully.

"You're sure you're not hurt?"

"No, I'm all right, thanks," replied Pinocchio, trying to pull away. He was still eager to get to school. But the wily Fox had other plans. He held the puppet back with his cane.

"Look, Gideon!" he exclaimed. "Do you see what I see?"

He turned Pinocchio around, admiring him from every angle, as though he had made a great discovery. "Look at that profile!" he cried. "And that figure! What a personality! My boy," he said, squeezing Pinocchio's hand, "let me congratulate you. You're a born actor. Your place is in the theatre!"

"Thank you," said Pinocchio, pleased. "But I have to go to school ––"

"School!" the Fox interrupted with a scornful laugh. "Of course, my boy — but later! Your career comes first. Why, I can see you now. The crowded house . . . the lights grow dim . . . the curtain rises . . ." Dramatically Foulfellow raised his cape. *"To be or not to be,"* he recited soulfully. "Ah, Hamlet — the immortal Hamlet!"

It did not take the clever Fox long to persuade Pinocchio to forget about school. As Jiminy Cricket came hurrying up, imagine how shocked he was to see Pinocchio with those rascals.

"Slickers!" the wise little cricket exclaimed. "No good will come of this. Hey, Pinoke! That's not the way to school!"

Though he called frantically, Pinocchio did not hear him. Instead, off he went with his new-found friends.

Jiminy gave a gigantic hop which landed him on Foulfellow's hat, where he finally got Pinocchio's attention.

"It's about time!" snorted Jiminy. "Now you listen to me for a while. Remember, I'm your conscience! You'd better take my advice, turn around and go to school!"

"But, Jiminy," argued the foolish puppet, "my place is in the theatre! Mr. Honest John told me so!"

"Honest John!" repeated Jiminy. "Who's that?"

"Him!" Pinocchio answered, pointing to the Fox. "His name is J. Worthington Foulfellow. The J. stands for John, Honest John. He's my friend. He's going to help me to be a success!"

"Don't believe all you hear," Jiminy warned. "Son, those fellows are a couple of ill winds in cheap clothing! You tell Honest John you're not going to be an actor. Tell him you're going to school, to work hard and become a real boy."

Pinocchio didn't know what to do. He looked from Jiminy to Foulfellow. The Fox beckoned impatiently.

"Come, my boy!" he announced. "There is no time to lose. We are off to fame and fortune!"

Fame and fortune! The words were too much for Pinocchio. "Good-by, Jiminy!" he called, and away he went with the Fox and Cat, leaving the little cricket puzzled and angry.

IMINY was not the only one who was disappointed. For an instant the Blue Fairy appeared in a circle of golden light. "Poor Pinocchio," she sighed. "So soon!"

Then she disappeared. The spot where she had stood became only a pool of limpid sunlight. Jiminy, sitting forlornly nearby, did not even see her.

"That boy!" he muttered. "He's burning his britches at both ends! But what can I do? Run and tell his father? . . . No — he wouldn't believe me. Call the police? . . . No — it's too late for that. Why don't you follow him?"

He stood up, clicked his heels together and answered his own question. "By gosh, I *will!*" he decided.

But Jiminy's little heart was heavy. He felt certain Pinocchio was about to ruin his chances of ever becoming a real boy. He kept thinking about old Geppetto.

That day the old woodcarver worked harder than he had ever done in his life. When the other children passed by on their way home he peered anxiously out. His little wooden boy was not among them.

"Oh, well," he told Figaro laughingly, "perhaps he was naughty and his teacher made him stay after school.

He cooked a delicious supper, and set the table with china dishes and tin knives and forks in Pinocchio's honor. Twilight fell, and still Pinocchio did not appear.

Had it not been for the fact that Geppetto was a stay-at-home, he would have known where Pinocchio was. For by now the whole village was plastered with posters advertising Stromboli's Marionette Show: "See Stromboli's NEW wonder puppet — PINOCCHIO THE GREAT!"

Yes. The plot of the greedy Fox had succeeded beyond his finest dreams. Foulfellow had gone to Stromboli and told him of this wonder puppet which could walk and talk without the aid of strings. Stromboli had agreed to purchase him if what Foulfellow said was true.

So the Fox summoned the Cat to show Pinocchio to the puppet-master. Stromboli examined him and found that everything the rogues claimed was true. Pinocchio was a live puppet; he could walk and talk without the aid of strings. Stromboli rubbed his hands together greedily.

"Congratulations, Maestro!' said Foulfellow. "I was sure you would appreciate this young man's talent. My boy, congratulations to you as well! Wait for

me without —"

He pushed Pinocchio and the Cat outside.

"I will buy him," said Stromboli, reaching inside his blouse. "Here! Two hundred —"

"Not enough." Foulfellow shook his head sadly.

"I'm a poor man!" Stromboli groaned. "Three hundred —?"

"Only three hundred, for that paragon of puppetry, that miracle of marionettes?" Foulfellow laughed scornfully. "My good man, no wonder you are poor. You don't know a good thing when you see one. Good-by."

But before the scoundrel got out, Stromboli gave him a fat sack of gold, which the Fox counted and hid carefully under his cape. Outside he and the Cat bade Pinocchio the fondest of farewells and went away.

Thus Pinocchio, never realizing that he had been sold into a life of slavery, joined Stromboli's Marionette Show.

IT WAS Stromboli's custom to travel wherever he chose, carrying his marionettes and crew in wagons, like a gypsy caravan. Here business had been very slow; the caravan was scheduled to move on soon. But with this new attraction — this wonder puppet, Pinocchio — things might be different!

So today Stromboli set the stage (which was simply one of his wagons with the side let down to form a narrow platform) with more than usual care. Everything was set for a gala performance.

When night fell a gay crowd collected in the Square. A record audience was on hand for the debut of Pinocchio the Great. Of course Jiminy came early. The curious little cricket chose a front seat on a lamp post near the stage. He didn't want to miss a thing.

Maestro Stromboli, dressed in a tight-fitting velvet suit, appeared and raised his baton. The band began to play. The show was on!

Out came the usual wooden marionettes, to go jerkily through their little acts. The audience clapped half-heartedly. This was not what they had come to see.

"Where is the wonder puppet?" they began grumbling. Finally a voice cried, "Bring on Pinocchio!"

Stromboli signaled his helpers to empty the stage.

"Ladees and gentullmen!" he proclaimed. "Now comes the most sensational act of my show! I give you the miracle marionette of the ages — a puppet who dances and sings without the aid of strings! Imported from the four corners of the universe — the great and only PINOCCHIO!"

"Boo! Boo!" cried the audience, for they did not believe there could be such a marionette anywhere in the world. But the curtain rose, and there stood — Pinocchio!

For an instant the audience suspected a trick. Then the marionette moved. He walked to the footlights. He was alive! And he had no strings.

Pinocchio was frightened by all those curious faces, but Stromboli motioned to him. "Sing!" he commanded. "Sing!"

Pinocchio swallowed hard and bravely began to sing:

> "I've no strings to hold me down,
> To make me fret and make me frown.
> I once had strings but now I'm free –
> There are no strings on me!
> Heigh-ho, the merry-o,
> What a pleasant way to be –
> Heigh-ho, the merry-o,
> There are no strings on me!"

When Pinocchio finished, the audience broke into wild cheers. "More! More!" they shouted enthusiastically.

Stromboli grinned. The applause was music to his ears. Jiminy was so surprised he nearly fell off his seat!

Once more the music began. Other puppets were pulled out on strings to join Pinocchio. There were tiny Dutch girl puppets who rolled their eyes, and French girls who flirted outrageously. There were Russian puppets who danced like whirling dervishes, and cannibal puppets who came out and did a whooping war dance.

But always Pinocchio danced in the spotlight, the star of the show. Jiminy Cricket felt very sheepish. Had he given Pinocchio the wrong advice? Perhaps the Fox and Cat were right, and the theatre *was* the road to success!

"Bravo! Bravissimo! Pinocchio!" the audience

 shouted, and showers of money fell on the stage about the puppet's feet.

Jiminy Cricket was convinced now that he had been a fool.

"Well, that's that," he said sadly. "He won't need me any more. What does an actor want with a conscience?"

So the little cricket, certain that his job was over, walked away, the applause still ringing in his ears.

WHEN at last the crowd realized the show was over and went home, Stromboli lifted Pinocchio up and kissed him on both cheeks.

"Bravo! Bravissimo!" he cried. "Pinocchio, you are a great actor! You are a sensation. I love you dearly!"

"Thank you," replied Pinocchio shyly. "I'm very glad. But now I must go."

"Go?" Stromboli repeated. "Go? Where must you go, my little friend?"

"Why, home, of course," answered Pinocchio. "I must tell my father what has happened. He doesn't know where I am."

Now that the excitement was over, Pinocchio realized suddenly that he was homesick. For the first time that day, the selfish puppet thought of his poor old father.

But when he spoke of home, Stromboli began to laugh loudly. "Ha ha ha!" he roared. "This is very comical!"

Suddenly he stopped laughing and a scowl blackened his face. He picked Pinocchio up, opened the door of a large bird cage and thrust him roughly inside. Then he locked the cage door and placed the key safely in his pocket.

"There!" he growled. "This is your home! You belong to _me!_ This town is too small for us. We will tour the world. London, Monte Carlo, Constantinople –"

"No, no!" cried Pinocchio. "I don't want to go to Constantinople. I want to go home!"

"Quiet, little one," Stromboli advised. "You will never see your home again. But you will make lots of money — for _me!_"

"No, no!" begged Pinocchio. "I don't want to be an actor! Let me out! I'll tell my father!"

"Foolish one, be still," Stromboli chuckled. "When you wake tomorrow, you will be far away! But you will learn to like this life. And when you grow too old to sing and dance, you will make good firewood. Look!"

He pointed to a wood box in the corner. To Pinocchio's horror, he recognized the sticks as parts of wooden marionettes — legs, arms, even heads — broken and useless.

"Let me out!" he screamed. But Stromboli only laughed and left the wagon.

Pinocchio began to cry bitterly. Between sobs he could hear rain pattering dismally on the roof. Then he heard the creak of wheels, and realized they were already leaving!

The lifeless marionettes hanging about the wagon swung mournfully back and forth. Pinocchio eyed them through his tears, realizing he was no better off than they. Once he had had a chance to become a real boy, but now . . . He buried his face in his hands.

As the caravan rumbled off through the quiet village old Geppetto, who was out searching for his lost son, saw it pass. But it was the last place he would have thought of looking for Pinocchio.

Cold and dejected, he padded along peering into every window and doorway. He even searched the waterfront, but the only person he saw was a policeman standing on a rain-swept wharf.

The policeman stared curiously at the funny old man.

"I'm looking for my son," explained Geppetto, "a puppet about so high —"

The policeman shook his head. "Crazy as a loon," he said to himself as he watched the old man disappear in the fog.

JIMINY sat dejectedly in the Square, rain dripping in torrents from his tiny umbrella. The little cricket wanted very much to go and congratulate Pinocchio, but he felt a bit timid.

When he saw Stromboli's caravan start away,

he felt very sad indeed, for he had learned to love Pinocchio dearly.

"There he goes, sitting in the lap of luxury," he said. "The world at his feet. Pinocchio the Great! Well," he sighed, "I can always say 'I knew him when'."

But still he was not resigned.

"I suppose it's better this way," he tried to tell himself. "I'll just go out of his life quietly. But I'd like to wish him luck for old times' sake . . . Well, why not?" he decided suddenly. "I may get thrown out — but here goes!"

Imagine his surprise when he saw the great actor a prisoner in a birdcage! Pinocchio was glad to see his tiny friend, and poured all his troubles into Jiminy's ear.

The cricket didn't even say, "I told you so."

"Never you mind, son," he told Pinocchio. "I'll get you out in no time. I didn't live in a hardware store two years for nothing." And he tried to pick the lock of the birdcage.

But try as he might, Jiminy was unable to release Pinocchio. "It would take a miracle to get us out of this he admitted finally and hopped back into the cage.

They huddled together in the dim, swaying wagon.

"I did so want to be a real boy," thought Pinocchio.

I did so want that gold badge," mourned Jiminy. Then he

saw that Pinocchio was really crying. "There, there, son," he comforted him. "Take it easy! Be cheerful, like me!"

He pointed to a small, high window in the wagon. "The rain has stopped, anyway," he said. "Hey — *look!*"

For just then the dark clouds parted and the Evening Star shone through. It seemed to be coming closer . . . .

"It's the Blue Fairy!" whispered Pinocchio. "What shall I tell her?" The dim wagon became brighter every second.

Just then, in her circle of light, the Blue Fairy appeared. "Why didn't you go to school, Pinocchio?" she asked.

Pinocchio blushed and stammered. Finally, "Well," he

said, "I was going to school when I met somebody." Then he hesitated.

"Yes?" prompted the Fairy.

"I met — two big monsters — with green eyes!"

Jiminy Cricket whistled warningly; he could see danger ahead. But Pinocchio went right on.

"They chased me with an axe," he said, "and they tied me up in a big sack —"

"And where was Sir Jiminy all this time?" interrupted the Blue Fairy.

"Jiminy? Why — ah — they tied him up in a little sack!"

And with that, Pinocchio's nose began to grow. It was very frightening, but Pinocchio couldn't stop lying. He added pirates, cannibals and Indians to his story. The more he embroidered his adventures, the more his nose grew, till it reached through the cage and clear across the wagon.

Finally he gave up, and whimpered, "My nose! What's happened?"

"Perhaps you haven't been telling the truth," suggested the Blue Fairy.

"Oh, but I *have* — every word!" vowed Pinocchio.

With that, bark began to grow on that long, funny nose.

Twigs and leaves branched out here and there. Finally at the very tip of it, Pinocchio could see a bird's nest. He felt very ridiculous and ashamed.

"Tell her the truth," advised Jiminy in a whisper.

"Well, to tell the truth," Pinocchio admitted sheepishly, "I *wasn't* telling the truth."

And with that, nest, bark, twigs and leaves all disappeared, and Pinocchio's nose grew back to its usual length. The Blue Fairy reached over and gave it a little tweak.

"You see, Pinocchio," she told him, "a lie grows and grows until it is as plain as the nose on your face."

Pinocchio was miserably unhappy. "I'll never lie again," he murmured.

"That's fine!" The Fairy smiled. "Now, how would you like to go home?"

"Home? Oh, boy!" shouted Pinocchio. Then his face fell. "I only wish I could," he said sadly.

"I will help you this time, Pinocchio," said the Blue Fairy. "Because you are truly sorry, you deserve one last chance. But if you fail again, you may never become a real boy!"

She touched the cage with her wand, the door swung open and Pinocchio was free. The wagon faded away, and he found

himself standing under the stars. Stromboli's caravan rolled
down the road without him. Pinocchio looked around.
The Blue Fairy was gone!

"She's a mighty fine lady, son," said Jiminy. "Now
remember what she said. This is your last chance!"

"I'm going straight home and start all over again," vowed
Pinocchio. "I'll go to school, study hard and try to become a
real boy. I've learned my lesson!"

PINOCCHIO was anxious now to see his father.
"Let's have a race!" he challenged Jiminy. "Last one home
is a ham actor!" And he began to run like the wind.

"All right!" Away went the little cricket at top speed, and Pinocchio was soon left far behind.

By chance the way home led through a dingy section near the waterfront, past a disreputable tavern called the Red Lobster Inn. Good people of the town turned their heads whenever they passed its doors, for the Red Lobster was where rogues and thieves met to plot their crimes and squander their ill-gotten riches.

Tonight Foulfellow and Gideon had a sumptuous meal at the Red Lobster Inn. Time after time, they raised their steins in a toast to their little wooden friend, Pinocchio. Toward the end of the evening, they were joined by a jovial Coachman who asked what they were celebrating.

The jubilant Fox told him the whole story.

"We sold the puppet to Stromboli, and believe me, he paid plenty!" He sifted a small pile of coins through his fingers.

The Coachman laughed scornfully. "Do you call *that* money?" he jeered. "Wait till you hear what I have to offer."

"We're terribly busy these days," drawled the Fox. "Still, your proposition might be amusing. What is it?"

The Coachman peered around to make sure he would not be overheard. But at this late hour the Red Lobster was almost deserted, so he began to unfold his sinister scheme.

"I'm looking for boys," he explained. "Stupid, good-for-nothing boys — the kind who play hookey from school. For every one you bring me, I'll pay cash. I load 'em on a coach and take 'em away to . . ." his voice sank to a whisper, "to *Pleasure Island!*"

Even Foulfellow and Gideon seemed somewhat shocked as the Coachman disclosed the fate of boys who went to Pleasure Island.

"Sounds dangerous," objected the Fox. "How about The Law?"

The Coachman shook his head. "There's not a chance of our getting caught," he said darkly. "You see, my dear Foulfellow . . . they never come back — *as boys!*" For an in-

stant that jovial face
changed, as though the
Coachman had donned
a mask of cruelty.
"Well – what do you say?"

The Cat looked scared
to death. But the Fox was
bolder. "We'll do it," he
agreed, "as long as there's money in it!"

"Good!" said the Coachman, rising to his feet. "The
coach leaves the Crossroads at midnight. Meet me there."

"At the Crossroads at midnight!"

Solemnly the Fox and Cat raised their steins, drank
and took leave of the Coachman. Just as they came out

of the Inn to begin their search for lazy, stupid boys, who should they see approaching but Pinocchio!

WHEN the Fox and Cat spied Pinocchio, their first impulse was to run.

"Wait!" muttered Foulfellow. "We'll sell *him* to the Coachman! Gideon, leave this to me!"

So once again the villains plotted to profit by the puppet's innocence.

"Pinocchio!" the Fox exclaimed. "What a pleasure to meet you! How is the great actor this evening?"

"I'm not an actor," Pinocchio retorted, "and I'm going home to my father. I'm going to school and study hard." He tried to get away, but Foulfellow pulled him back.

"What about Stromboli?" he asked.

"Stromboli was awful. He put me in a cage!"

Foulfellow and Gideon looked shocked.

"How terrible!" they murmured, and, "It's un-believable!"

"Well, it's true," said Pinocchio. "I had an awful time."

This gave the Fox a

bright idea. "Why, my boy, you must be a nervous wreck!" he exclaimed. He bent over, took Pinocchio's pulse, and raised his eyebrows in alarm. "We must diagnose your case immediately," he announced.

"But I have to go to school and —"

"Certainly!" interrupted the Fox.

"But you can't possibly go to school in this terrible state," and he pretended to examine Pinocchio all over. Then he took a long breath.

"You have a slight touch of monetary complications of the flying trapezius, plus a compound transaction of the pandemonium," he began. "In addition, you show symptoms of palpitation syncopation of the killer-diller, and a bucolic semilunar contraption . . . together with a touch of sagacious prognostication of the basic rathbone!"

Pinocchio began to look very worried, and the Fox soon convinced him he was at death's door.

"Now that we know the worst," he said, "we must find a remedy! Pinocchio, you need a vacation on Pleasure Island!"

"Pleasure Island?" repeated Pinocchio.

"Pleasure Island!" cried Foulfellow. "Where every day is a holiday, with fireworks, brass bands, parades — a paradise for boys! Why, I can see you now — lolling under a doughnut tree, a lollipop in each hand, gazing off at the pink Ice Cream Mountains — think of it, Pinocchio!"

It was a tempting picture the sly Fox painted, "Well, I *was* going to school," Pinocchio hesitated. "But perhaps I could go to Pleasure Island first — for a little while . . ."

Thus again he forgot all his good resolutions and started away arm-in-arm with his false friends.

Meanwhile, Jiminy Cricket, still thinking he was racing Pinocchio home, arrived at Geppetto's doorstep. When he  turned around and the puppet was nowhere to be seen, he started back to look for him.

It was almost midnight when he reached the Crossroads. There he saw that Pinocchio had once more fallen into the hands of the Fox and Cat. They were loading him onto a great stagecoach, piled to the brim with boys — eager, noisy, impudent boys!

"Good-by!" Pinocchio called. "I'll never be able to thank you for this!"

"Think nothing of it, my boy," said the Fox. "Seeing you happy is our only reward. Our only reward — reward — *reward!*" he kept repeating, until the Coachman slipped him a large sack of gold. He hid the gold under his cape, and disappeared into the woods. The Coachman cracked his long blacksnake whip, and the coach started to move.

It was drawn by twelve sorrowful looking little donkeys, who seemed to feel very badly about the whole thing. "Tsk! Tsk! Tsk!" they said, every time the Coachman's whip descended. But nobody could hear them because of the boys' shouting.

"Three cheers for anything," they yelled, throwing their caps into the air. "Hurray for Pleasure Island!"

Jiminy made a last desperate effort. He hopped onto the rear axle of the coach and rode along. Certain Pinocchio was once more headed for disaster, the loyal little cricket went with him just the same.

THE JOURNEY was an unhappy one for Jiminy. At the waterfront, the passengers boarded a ferry boat for Pleasure Island, and the little cricket suffered from seasickness during the entire voyage.

But physical discomfort was not what bothered him most. He was worried about Pinocchio, who promptly made friends

with the worst boy in the crowd — a no-good named "Lamp-wick." Lampwick talked out of the corner of his mouth, and was very untidy. Yet Pinocchio cherished his friendship.

Jiminy tried to warn Pinocchio, but the heedless puppet refused to listen. Finally the ferry docked and the boys swarmed down the gangplank onto Pleasure Island.

Bands played loudly; wonderful circuses performed along the streets, which were paved with cookies and lined with doughnut trees. Lollipops and cup-cakes grew on bushes, and fountains spouted lemonade and soda pop. The Mayor of Pleasure Island made a speech of welcome and urged the boys to enjoy themselves.

Yes, Pleasure Island seemed to be all the Fox had claimed for it, and more. Only Jiminy Cricket was skeptical.

He felt that there was more to all this than appeared on the surface. But weeks went by, and seldom did Jiminy get close enough to Pinocchio to warn him. He was always in the midst of the fun, and his friend Lampwick was the ringleader of the horde of carefree, mischievous boys.

They smashed windows and burned school books; in fact they did whatever they felt like doing, no matter how destructive. They ate until they nearly burst. And always the Coachman and Mayor encouraged them to "Have a good time — while you can!"

And all the while the poor little donkeys — who performed all the hard labor on the island — looked very sad and said "Tsk! Tsk! Tsk!"

One day Pinocchio and Lampwick were lazily floating in a canoe along the Lemonade River, which flowed between the Ice Cream Mountains. Chocolate cattails grew thickly along the banks, lollipop trees drooped overhead and the canoe was piled high with sweets.

"This is too good to be true, Lampwick," Pinocchio sighed blissfully. "I could stay here forever!"

"Aw, this is kid stuff," retorted Lampwick. "Let's go where we can have some real fun!"

"Where?" asked Pinocchio curiously.

"I'll show you," said Lampwick. So they pulled the canoe up on the bank, and Lampwick led the way to Tobacco Lane.

Here the fences were made of cigars, cigarettes and matches grew on bushes, and there were rows of cornstalks with corncob pipes on them. Lampwick lit a cigar and began smoking.

Pinocchio hesitated. Finally he picked a corncob pipe and began to puff timidly.

"Aw, you smoke like my grandmudder," jeered Lampwick. "Take a big drag, Pinoke — like dis!"

Under Lampwick's instruction, Pinocchio soon found himself smoking like a chimney. Just then, along came Jiminy. How sad the little cricket felt when he saw this you will never know.

WHILE he had known for a long time that Pinocchio had fallen into evil ways, Jiminy did not realize he had sunk to such depths.

Well, he had tried everything — except force. Would that make the lad come to his senses? He decided to try. He shook his little fist angrily. "So it's come to this, has it?" he shouted. "SMOKING!"

Pinocchio gave him a careless glance. "Yeah," he answered out of the corner of his mouth, in imitation of Lampwick. "So what?"

"Just this!" Jiminy exploded. "You're making a disgusting spectacle of yourself. You're going home this minute!"

Lampwick, who had never seen Jiminy before, was curious. "Who's de insect, Pinoke?" he asked.

"Jiminy? Why, he's my conscience," explained Pinocchio.

Lampwick began to laugh. "You mean you take advice from a *beetle?*" he remarked insultingly. "Say, I can't waste time wid a sap like you. So long!" And he strolled away.

"Lampwick! Don't go!" cried Pinocchio. "Now see what you've done, Jiminy! Lampwick was my best friend!"

That was too much for the little cricket. "So *he's* your best friend," he said angrily. "Well, Pinocchio, that's the last straw. I'm through! I'm taking the next boat out of here!"

Pinocchio hesitated but temptation was too strong. He couldn't give Lampwick up. He started off after him, full of apologies.

"Hey, wait, Lampwick!" he called. "I'm coming with *you!*"

That was the end as far as Jiminy was concerned. "So he prefers to remain with that hoodlum, and allow him to insult *me,* his conscience?" he muttered. "Well, from now on he can paddle his own canoe. I'm going home!"

And he started toward the entrance gate, so upset

that he did not notice how dark and forlorn Pleasure Island looked. There wasn't a boy in sight on the wide streets.

Jiminy's only thought was to get away quickly. He was just about to pound angrily on the gate when he heard voices on the other side. He tried to listen, and became conscious of a reddish glow which cast great, frightening shadows against the high stone walls. The shadows looked like prison guards, and they carried guns!

Jiminy jumped up and peered fearfully through the keyhole. In the cove, lit by flaming torches, he saw something that made his blood turn cold.

The ferry boat stood waiting, stripped of its decorations. The dock swarmed with howling, braying donkeys — fat ones and thin ones, many of whom still wore boys' hats and shoes. Huge, ape-like guards herded them into crates, assisted by the Coachman who cracked his whip brutally over the poor donkeys' heads.

The little cricket shuddered. At last he understood the meaning of Pleasure Island. This, then, was what became of lazy, good-for-nothing boys! They made donkeys of themselves! This was Pinocchio's fate, unless —

Forgetting his anger, Jiminy leaped to the ground and started back toward Tobacco Lane. He must warn Pinocchio to leave at once.

"Pinocchio!" he yelled. "Pinocchio!" But his cries only echoed through the empty streets.

Not far away, Pinocchio was still looking for Lampwick. He wandered unhappily past pie trees and popcorn shrubs. The island suddenly seemed strange, deserted.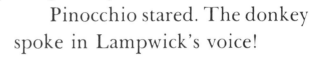

Then he heard a frightened voice say, "Here I am!"

"Lampwick!" Pinocchio answered joyfully. "Where are you?"

Just then a little donkey emerged from some bushes. "Ssh!" he whispered. "Stop yelling! They'll hear us!"

Pinocchio stared. The donkey spoke in Lampwick's voice!

"This is no time for jokes," Pinocchio said crossly. "What are you doing in that donkey suit?"

"This ain't no donkey suit, Pinoke," the frightened voice replied. "I *am* a donkey!"

Pinocchio laughed. "You a donkey?" For he still thought it was a joke. "Ha ha ha! *He-Haw! He-Haw! He-Haw!*"

Pinocchio turned pale, but he couldn't stop. He was braying like a donkey! He put his hand over his mouth.

The little donkey came closer to him. "That's the first sign of donkey fever," he whispered. "That's how I started."

"Then — you *are* Lampwick! What happened?"

"Donkey fever," replied Lampwick, "and you've got it too!"

Pinocchio's head began to buzz like a hive of bees. He reached up and felt something horrible. Two long, hairy ears were growing out of his head!

"You've got it all right!" whispered Lampwick. "Look behind you!"

Pinocchio looked and discovered that he had a long tail. He began to tremble, and was no longer able to stand up straight. Then he found himself on all fours, like a donkey!

"Help! Help!" he shrieked. "Jiminy! Jiminy Cricket!"

Jiminy ran toward them, but he saw that he was too late.

"Oh! Oh! Oh me, oh my!" he groaned. "Look at you! Come on! Let's get away from here before you're a complete donkey!"

This time nobody argued with the little cricket. As he fled toward the high stone wall, Pinocchio and the donkey that had once been Lampwick followed as fast as their legs would carry them. But as they rounded a corner, they came face to face with the Coachman and his armed guards. They turned and dashed toward the opposite wall.

"There they go! That's the two that's missing!" yelled the Coachman. "After them! Sound the alarm!"

Instantly the air was filled with the sound of sirens and the baying of bloodhounds. Searchlights began to play over the island, and bullets whizzed past the ears of the escaping prisoners. They expected any minute to be shot.

Pinocchio and Jiminy reached the wall and managed to climb to the top before the ape-like guards

got within shooting distance. But Pinocchio looked down, and saw a little donkey choking and kicking as he was caught with a rope lasso. It was Lampwick.

"Go on, Pinoke!" he cried. "It's all over with me!"

A lump came in Pinocchio's throat. After all, Lampwick was his friend. But there was nothing he could do. He turned his back and said a silent prayer. Then he and Jiminy dove into the sea.

Bullets splashed all around them in the water, but by some miracle neither of them was hit. Finally a thick fog hid them from the glaring searchlights, and the sound of the guns died away. They had escaped!

IT WAS a long, hard swim back to the mainland. When they reached shore, they were by no means at the end of their journey, for home was still many weary miles away.

Pinocchio longed to see once more the cozy little cottage and his dear, kind father. Pleasure Island, and all it stood for, now seemed like a bad dream. The worst was over!

But as time wore on, Pinocchio found that this was not true. His long donkey ears and ridiculous

tail made him the object of jeers and laughter. Everywhere he went, people pointed him out and stared at him. Finally he could stand it no longer.

"We'll do our traveling after dark," he told Jiminy.

So from then on, Pinocchio and Jiminy walked at night. In the daytime they hid in dog houses and lived on crusts and bones. The autumn wind chilled them, for their clothes were worn; they were even forced to stuff old newspapers inside their thin shoes.

It was winter when at last one evening they limped into the village. They hurried through the drifting snow to Geppetto's shop. Pinocchio pounded on the door with eager fists.

"Father! Father!" he cried. "It's me! It's Pinocchio!"

But the only reply was the howling of the wintry wind.

"He must be asleep," said Pinocchio, and he knocked again. But again there was no answer.

Worried, Pinocchio hastened to the window and peered in. The house was empty! Everything was shrouded and dusty.

"He's gone, Jiminy," said Pinocchio sorrowfully. "My father's gone away!"

"Looks like he's gone for good, too," said Jiminy. "What'll we do?"

"I don't know." Pinocchio sat down on the doorstep, shivering. A tear came from his eye, ran down his long nose and froze into a tiny, sparkling icicle. But Pinocchio didn't even bother to wipe it off. He felt terrible.

Just then a gust of wind blew around the corner, carrying a piece of paper. Jiminy hopped over to see what it was.

"Hey, Pinoke, it's a letter!" he exclaimed.

"Oh! Maybe it's from my father!" cried Pinocchio, and he quickly took the note from Jiminy and tried to read it. But alas, the marks on the paper meant nothing to him.

"You see, if you had gone to school you could read your father's letter," Jiminy reminded him. "Here – give it to me!"

The little cricket began to read the note aloud, and this is what it said:

"Dear Pinocchio:

I heard you had gone to Pleasure Island, so I got a small boat and started off to search for you. Everyone said it was a dangerous voy-

age, but Figaro, Cleo and I thought we could reach you and save you from a terrible fate.

"We weathered the storms, and finally reached the Terrible Straits. But just as we came in sight of our goal, out of the sea rose Monstro, the Terror of the Deep—the giant whale who swallows ships whole. He opened his jaws. In we went — boat and all . . . "

Here Pinocchio's sobs interrupted Jiminy's reading of the letter as he realized Geppetto's plight.

"Oh, my poor, poor father!" the puppet moaned. "He's dead! And it's all my fault!" He began to weep bitterly.

"But he isn't dead!" said Jiminy, and read on.

"So now, dear son, we are living at the bottom of the ocean in the belly of the whale. But there is very little to eat here, and we cannot exist much longer. So I fear you will never again see

Your loving father,
GEPPETTO."

HURRAH! HURRAH!" shouted Pinocchio.

"Hurrah for what?" asked Jiminy somewhat crossly. It did not seem to him to be quite the time for cheers.

"Don't you see, Jiminy?" cried Pinocchio. "My father is still alive! There may be time to save him!"

"Save him?" said Jiminy stupidly. Then suddenly a light

dawned. "You don't mean *you* —"

"Yes!" announced Pinocchio. "I'm going after him. It's my fault he's down there in the whale; I'm going to the bottom of the ocean and rescue him!"

"But Pinocchio, you might be killed!" warned the cricket.

"I don't mind," declared Pinocchio. "What does life mean to me without my father? I've got to save him!"

Jiminy stared with open mouth. He hardly recognized this new Pinocchio—a brave, unselfish Pinocchio who stood there in place of the weak, foolish puppet he had always known.

"But think how far it is to the seashore —" he began.

Pinocchio looked thoughtful, but not for long. "I don't care. No place is too far for me to go after my father."

Just then, with a flutter of wings, a beautiful white dove settled gracefully down in the snow beside them.

"I will take you to the seashore," she said softly.

"You?" Pinocchio stared. But he did not see the tiny gold crown on the dove's head. It was she who had dropped the letter from the sky. She was his own dear Blue Fairy, disguised as a dove.

"Yes, I will help you," she assured him.

"How could a little dove carry me to the seashore?"

"Like this!"

And the dove began to grow and grow, until she was larger than an eagle. "Jump on my back," she commanded. Pinocchio obeyed.

"Good-by, Jiminy Cricket," he said. "I may never see you again." He waved his hand to his little friend. "Thank you for all you've done!"

"Good-by, nothing!" retorted Jiminy, and he too jumped on the back of the great white dove. "You're not leaving me! We'll see this through together!"

The dove raised her wide wings and rose from the ground. Higher and higher they flew, till the village disappeared and all they could see beneath them was whirling snow.

All night they flew through the storm. When morning came, the sun shone brightly. The dove's wings slowed down and she glided to earth at the edge of a cliff. Far below, the sea lay churning and lashing like a restless giant.

"I can take you no farther," said the dove. "Are you quite

sure you want to go on this dangerous mission?"

"Yes," said Pinocchio. "Thank you for the ride. Good-by!"

"Good-by, Pinocchio," the dove replied. "Good luck!"

And she grew small again and flew away. Neither Pinocchio nor Jiminy realized that she was the Blue Fairy, but they were very grateful.

A S SOON as the dove was out of sight, Pinocchio tied a big stone to his donkey tail, to anchor him to the floor of the ocean. Then he smiled bravely at Jiminy, who smiled back, and together they leaped off the cliff.

The weight of the stone caused Pinocchio to sink at once. By clinging desperately, little Jiminy managed to stay close by. They landed, picked themselves up and peered about. They were at the very bottom of the sea.

At first it seemed dark; they were many fathoms deep. Gradually Pinocchio's eyes became accustomed to the greenish light which filtered down into the submarine forest.

Giant clumps of seaweed waved overhead, like the branches of trees. Among them darted lovely, bright objects, like birds or living flowers. They soon saw that these brilliant creatures were fish of all descriptions.

However, Pinocchio was in no frame of mind to make a study of the citizens of the sea. He walked along, peering into every cave and grotto in search of the great whale. But the stone attached to his tail made him move slowly, and he grew impatient.

"I wish we knew just where to look," he thought. "Jiminy, where do you suppose Monstro might be?"

"Don't know, I'm sure," replied Jiminy. "But we might ask some of these — er, people. I'll inquire here."

He knocked politely on an oyster. Its shell opened.

"Pardon me, Pearl," Jiminy began, "but could you tell me where we might find Monstro the Whale?"

To his surprise, the shell closed with a sharp click and the oyster scuttled off into a kelp bush as though frightened.

"Hm! That's funny!" remarked Jiminy.

Just then a school of tropical fish approached, brightly beautiful and extremely curious.

"I wonder," Pinocchio began, "if you could tell me where to find Monstro—"

But the lovely little creatures darted away before he had finished speaking. It was as though Pinocchio had threatened to harm them in some way.

A bit farther along, they encountered a herd

of tiny sea horses, grazing on the sandy bottom. Pinocchio tried once more.

"Could you tell me," he asked, "where I might find Monstro the Whale?"

But the sea horses fled, their little ears raised in alarm.

"You know what I think?" exclaimed Jiminy. "I think everybody down here is afraid of Monstro! Why, they run away at the very mention of his name! He must be awful. Do you think we should go on?"

"Certainly!" declared Pinocchio. "I'm not afraid!"

So they went on. It was a strange journey. Sometimes the water grew very dark, and tiny phosphorescent fish glowed like fireflies in the depths. They learned to be careful not to

step on the huge flowers which lay on the ocean's floor. For they were not flowers but sea anemones, which could reach up and capture whatever came within their grasp.

Striped fish glared at them from seaweed thickets like tigers in a jungle, and fish with horns and quills glowered at them. They saw wonders of the deep which no human eye has ever beheld — but nowhere could they find so much as one clue to the whereabouts of Monstro, the Terror of the Deep.

"The time is getting short!" said Pinocchio at last. "We must find him! My father will starve to death! Father!" he cried desperately. "Father!"

But there was no sound except the constant shifting and sighing of the watery depths.

"Let's go home, Pinocchio," Jiminy pleaded.

"We'll never find Monstro in this big place. For all we know, we may be looking in the wrong ocean."

"No, Jiminy," said Pinocchio, "I'll never give up! Never!"

NOT FAR away lay the Terror of the Deep, floating close to the surface, fast asleep. At times his broad back rose out of the water, to be mistaken for a desert island.

It was lucky for any ship close by that Monstro slept, for with but one flip of his tail he had been known to crush the sturdiest craft. As he snored the roars sounded like a tempest. It seemed impossible that anything could live within those crushing jaws.

Yet at the far end of the long, dark cavern formed by the whale's mouth lived a strange household. A kindly old man, whose skin was as pale as white paper, a small black kitten whose ribs nearly pierced his fur, and a tiny, frightened gold-fish, who swam weakly around in her bowl.

The old woodcarver had constructed a rude home, fur-nished with broken packing-cases from ships the whale had swallowed. He had salvaged a lantern, pots and pans and a few other necessities of life. But his stock of food was now very low; the lantern sputtering above his table was almost out of oil. The end was near.

Every day he fished in the mouth of the whale; but when Monstro slept, nothing entered that dark cavern. Now there was only a shallow pool of water, and it was useless to fish.

"Not a bite for days, Figaro," Geppetto said. "If Monstro doesn't wake up soon, it will be too bad for us. I never thought it would end like this!" He sighed mournfully. "Here we are, starving in the belly of a whale. And Pinocchio—poor little Pinocchio!" Geppetto was obliged to raise his thin voice to a shout, to be heard above the whale's snoring.

The old woodcarver looked tired and worn. He had never been so hungry in his whole life. Figaro was hungry too. He stared greedily at little Cleo, swimming slowly about her bowl.

As Geppetto went wearily back to his fishing, the kitten began to sneak toward Cleo's bowl. But the old man saw him.

"Scat!" shouted Geppetto. "You beast! You *dog!* Shame on you, Figaro, chasing Cleo, after the way I've brought you up!"

The hungry kitten scuttled away to a corner to try to forget the pangs which gnawed him. Just then Geppetto felt a nibble at his line. He pulled it up in great excitement.

"It's a package, Figaro!" he cried. "Maybe it's food. Sausage, or cheese —"

But when the water-soaked package was unwrapped, it contained only a cook book! What a grim trick Fate had played!

"Oh, oh," groaned Geppetto. "I am so hungry! If only we had something to cook! Anything —"

He turned the pages, his mouth watering at the pictured recipes. "101 Ways to Cook Fish," he read. Suddenly his eyes were drawn, as if by a magnet, to Cleo. He could almost see the melted butter sizzling! As in a nightmare, he walked toward the goldfish bowl.

But as he started to scoop his little pet out and put her in the frying pan, the old man realized he could never do this thing.

"Dear Cleo," he begged, "forgive me! If we must die, let us die as we have lived — friends through thick and thin!"

It was a solemn moment. All felt that the end was near.

Then the whale moved!

"He's waking up!" cried Geppetto. "He's opening his mouth!"

Monstro gave an upward lunge, and through his jaws rushed a wall of black water. With it came fish — a whole school of fish! Hundreds of them.

"Food!" yelled Geppetto, seizing his pole. "Tuna fish! Oh, Figaro, Cleo — we are saved!"

And he began to pull fish after fish out of the water.

WHEN Monstro woke, opened his eyes and saw the school of tuna approaching, he threshed the ocean into turmoil for miles around.

Pinocchio noticed every creature in the sea taking flight, but he did not understand the reason until he saw the whale coming toward him. Then he *knew*.

"Monstro!" he shrieked. "Jiminy, swim for your life!" For although he had long been in search of the Terror of the

Deep, a mere look at those crushing jaws was enough to make him flee in terror.

But nothing in Monstro's path could escape. He swallowed hundreds of tuna at one gulp. Into that huge maw finally went Pinocchio!

At last, completely satisfied, the whale grunted and settled down in his watery bed for another nap.

"Blubber-mouth!" cried a small, shrill voice. "Let me in!"

It was Jiminy, clinging to an empty bottle, bobbing up and down outside Monstro's jaws, begging to be swallowed too.

But the whale paid no attention, except to settle farther into the water. The little cricket was left alone, except for a flock of seagulls, who began to swoop down and peck at him. He raised his umbrella and drove them away, got inside the bottle and prepared to wait for Pinocchio.

Inside the whale, although Geppetto's bin was already heaped, he was still at work pulling in tuna.

"There's enough food to last us for months," he told Figaro joyfully. "Wait, there's another big one!" He scarcely noticed a shrill little cry of "Father!"

"Pinocchio?" the old man asked himself in wonderment, and turned around. There, standing before him, was his boy!

"Pinocchio!" he exclaimed joyfully. "Are my eyes telling me the truth? Are you really my own dear Pinocchio?"

Geppetto was not the only one who was glad. Figaro licked Pinocchio's face, and little Cleo turned somersaults.

"You see, we have all missed you," said Geppetto fondly. "But you're sneezing! You've caught cold, son! You should not have come down here! Sit down and rest. Give me your hat!"

But when Pinocchio's hat was removed, those hated

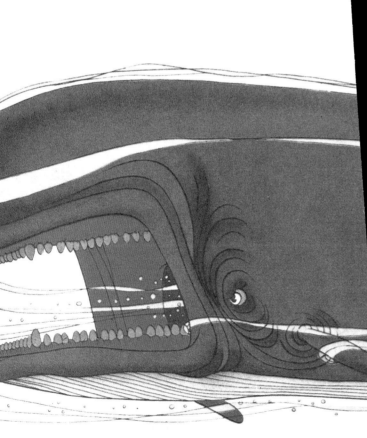

donkey ears popped out into plain sight.

"Pinocchio!" cried Geppetto, shocked. *"Those ears!"*

Pinocchio hung his head in shame. "I've got a tail, too," he admitted sadly. *"Oh, Father!"* And he turned his head away to hide his tears.

"Never mind, son," Geppetto comforted him. "The main thing is that we are all together again."

Pinocchio brightened up. "The *main* thing is to figure out a way to get out of this whale!"

"I've tried everything," said Geppetto hopelessly. "I even built a raft —"

"That's it!" cried Pinocchio. "When he opens his mouth, we'll float out on the raft!"

"Oh, no," argued Geppetto. "When he opens his mouth everything comes in — nothing goes out. Come, we are all hungry — I will cook a fish dinner! Help me build a fire —"

"That's it, Father!" interrupted Pinocchio. "We'll build a great big fire!" And he began to throw into the fire everything he could get his hands on.

"Not the chairs!" warned Geppetto. "What will we sit on?"

"We won't need chairs," shouted Pinocchio. "Father, don't you understand? We'll build a big fire and make Monstro sneeze! When he sneezes, out we go! Hurry — more wood!"

As the fire began to smoke they got the raft ready.

"It won't work, son," Geppetto insisted mournfully.

But before long the whale began to grunt and cough. Suddenly he drew in his breath and gave a monstrous SNEEZE!

Out went the raft, past those crushing jaws, into the sea.
"We made it!" shouted Pinocchio. "Father, we're free!'

BUT they were not yet free. The angry whale saw them, and plunged ferociously after their frail raft. He hit it squarely, splintering it into thousands of pieces. Pinocchio and Geppetto swam for their lives, with Monstro, the Terror of the Deep, in full pursuit.

The old man clung weakly to a board. He knew he could never reach land, but there was still hope for Pinocchio.

"Save yourself, my boy!" cried Geppetto. "Swim for shore, and don't worry about me!"

But the brave puppet swam to his father and managed to keep him afloat. Giant waves swept them toward the dark, forbidding rocks which lined the shore. Even if they escaped Monstro, they would surely be crushed to death.

But between two of the rocks there was a small, hidden crevice. By some miracle, Pinocchio and Geppetto were washed through this crevice into a small, sheltered lagoon. Again and again the furious whale threw his bulk against the rocks on the other side. His quarry had escaped!

But alas, when Geppetto sat up dizzily he saw poor Pinocchio lying motionless beside him, still and pale. The heartbroken old man knelt and wept bitterly, certain his wooden boy was dead.

The gentle waves carried a fishbowl up onto the beach. It was Cleo — and to the edge of the bowl clung a bedraggled kitten, Figaro. But even they were no comfort to Geppetto now.

A bottle bobbed up out of the water. Inside it rode Jiminy Cricket. He saw what had happened and longed to comfort Geppetto, but his own heart was broken.

The sorrowful old man finally gathered poor Pinocchio in his arms, picked up his pets and started home. They too felt sad, for they knew Geppetto was lonelier than he had ever been before.

When they reached home, it no longer seemed a home; it was dark and cheerless. Geppetto put Pinocchio on the workbench, buried his face in his hands and prayed.

Suddenly a ray of starlight pierced the gloom. It sought out the lifeless figure of the puppet. A voice which seemed to come from the sky said, as it had said once before:

"— and some day, when you have proven yourself brave,

truthful and unselfish, you will be a real boy —"

The old man saw and heard nothing. But Pinocchio stirred, sat up and looked around. He saw the others grieving, and wondered why. Then he looked down at himself, felt of his arms and legs, and suddenly he realized what had happened.

"Father!" he cried. "Father, look at me!"

Pinocchio was alive — really alive. No longer a wooden puppet, but a real flesh-and-blood boy!

Geppetto stared unbelievingly. Once more he picked Pinocchio up in his arms and hugged him, and cried — this time for joy. Again a miracle had been performed; this was truly the answer to his wish — the son he had always wanted!

What did they do to celebrate? Geppetto made a fire and soon the house was as warm and cozy as ever. He started all the clocks, and played the music box. Figaro turned somersaults, and Cleo raced madly about her bowl. Pinocchio flew to get his precious toys, even they seemed gayer than ever.

As for Jiminy Cricket, he was the happiest and proudest of all. For on his lapel he now wore a beautiful badge of shining gold!